MIS-STEAK-N IDENTITY

IRON & FLAME COZY MYSTERIES, BOOK 5

PATTI BENNING

SUMMER PRESCOTT BOOKS PUBLISHING

Copyright 2024 Summer Prescott Books

All Rights Reserved. No part of this publication nor any of the information herein may be quoted from, nor reproduced, in any form, including but not limited to: printing, scanning, photocopying, or any other printed, digital, or audio formats, without prior express written consent of the copyright holder.

**This book is a work of fiction. Any similarities to persons, living or dead, places of business, or situations past or present, is completely unintentional.

ONE

"You're going to be shadowing Noel today, so just relax and follow her lead. Don't hesitate to ask her if you have any questions."

Lydia Thackery gave Penny, one of their three new hires, an encouraging smile. Next to her, Noel, a server who had been with them almost from the beginning, nodded along in agreement with her words.

"Seriously, you can ask me anything, even if it seems like it's something that should be obvious. We were all newbies once, and I really enjoy doing the training. It gives me an excuse to stand around and chat instead of working my butt off. Don't tell the boss."

She winked at the end of her last sentence, and Lydia, who co-owned Iron and Flame with her ex-husband, made a show of pretending not to hear. Penny, who was a fresh high school graduate and looked deathly nervous on her first day at her first job, looked between the two of them uncertainly. Lydia decided to take pity on her and leave her in Noel's hands for the time being. She thought she was pretty laid back both as a boss and a chef, but the surge of hiring they had done over the past couple of weeks had made her realize that interacting with the restaurant's owners invariably made the new employees nervous.

They would come around; she was sure of it. Penny was the last of three hires; the other two included another server, a young man named Gabe who had worked at a chain restaurant before this, and a junior chef named Mira who was a recent grad from a small culinary school that had a great reputation.

Three new employees in as many weeks was a lot for a small steakhouse like Iron and Flame, but the success of their recent advertising campaign had made it a necessity. Her beloved restaurant was growing, and Lydia felt as proud as a new mother watching her toddler take his first steps.

She was in a good mood as she returned to the kitchen and finished the last few steps of her opening routine and began working on the first lunch order. Her good mood lasted until noon, when the swinging door to the kitchen opened and Jorge, the sous chef who was on shift with her this morning, said, "Good afternoon, Mr. Montrose."

Lydia, who was busy spooning melted butter and fresh thyme over a porterhouse steak on the griddle, paused long enough to glance over her shoulder and meet her ex-husband's eyes. She and Jeremy had an unwritten, unspoken rule; don't bother the other while they're working. He had the evening shift and wasn't supposed to be here until four thirty or so. She raised an eyebrow in a silent question before she returned her attention to the steak.

"I told you, just call me Jeremy," he said as he passed by Jorge. "Mr. Montrose makes me feel old and stuffy. Lydia, can you do me a favor?"

She flipped the steak, keeping most of her focus on that instead of on her ex-husband. Something in his tone made her suspicious, and she pressed her lips together for a moment before she answered.

"What is it?"

"I need you to cover my shift tonight, at least the last three hours of it. I misread the schedule—I'll take full blame for that—but I've got a date, and I really do not want to screw it up. I'll take the shift next Sunday that we argued over last week in exchange."

"You're dating again?" she asked. Jeremy went on a lot of dates... or, he used to, until one of the women he was seeing was murdered. He hadn't seen anyone since then, and it had been over half a year. While her ex-husband's dating life was none of her business, she was both surprised and happy to hear that he was back to feeling more like himself. She didn't *like* Jeremy very much most of the time, but that didn't mean she hated him, and she didn't like seeing him so depressed.

"I'm taking Melanie out," he said. "We both want something serious this time. I'm taking her out to that new seafood place in Wausau. I've got to get going, actually—still need to make the reservations and buy some flowers and all of that. Thanks, Lyd. I owe you one."

She had to take the steak off the griddle and set it down on a small wooden cutting board to rest before she could respond, and in those brief seconds,

Jeremy made his exit, clapping Jorge on the shoulder and then all but fleeing from the kitchen before giving her a chance to respond.

It was almost as if he could tell what her answer was going to be if he gave her a chance to give it.

"Can you plate this for me?" she asked Jorge, who looked like he was trying very hard not to get involved with his bosses' personal business. She didn't blame him; running a restaurant with her ex-husband was awkward enough for her. Her employees didn't have it much better, even though she and Jeremy usually made an effort not to let their squabbles spill over into the business side of things.

Her sous chef nodded, so she abandoned her post and rushed to follow Jeremy out of the kitchen. She was happy for him and Melanie, she really was—the two of them had been on and off for years, and even though it was a little strange if she stopped to think about it, Lydia actually got along with her quite well. On a different day, she probably would have been happy to cover his shift for him. Today was different, because today she had plans.

She spotted Jeremy across the restaurant and marched over to tell him he was going to need to figure something else out. He had almost made it to the door, but it looked like he had been waylaid by someone he knew. They were standing in front of the hostess' station, and poor Jaelin looked torn between asking them to move so she could help the next person in line and keeping quiet because she didn't want to tell one of the owners of the restaurant what to do.

Lydia had no such compunctions. "You're blocking the guests, Jeremy," she snapped once she reached them. "And I can't cover your shift tonight, you need to figure something else out."

"Hold on," he said over his shoulder to her, though he did guide the man he was talking to out of the way so Jaelin could seat the next couple in line.

Lydia followed him and his friend to a quieter corner by the door, not willing to let this go. She knew if he left, she would be out of luck; even if she called or texted him, he would just ignore his phone and pretend he hadn't seen it. Since he had gone to the effort of stopping in to ask—or rather, tell—her about taking his shift, she guessed he had already asked Hank and been turned down. Hank was semi-retired and worked for them only part-time and had been asking for fewer and fewer hours. She was hoping Mira, their new junior chef, would be prepared to take his place by the time he retired fully.

The man Jeremy was talking to glanced at her, then refocused on Jeremy. He had light brown hair that looked like it was beginning to grey early, and seemed to be around their age, in his thirties. He had pushed his glasses up his nose twice in the time since she joined them, and he seemed nervous.

"You know I wouldn't ask if I wasn't desperate. I can pay you back half the next time I get paid, and the rest next month."

"This is the third time you've needed my help, Tyler," Jeremy said.

"I know, but this is the last time, I swear. C'mon, man, you're the one who got me into poker. I wouldn't be in this position if it wasn't for you. Robert's serious about it, I don't think he's going to leave me alone until I pay up. I have until Sunday to get him the money, that's when he goes back home. I'm in real trouble if I don't have it by then."

Jeremy sighed. "I'll think about it, all right? Give me a call later tonight. This isn't a good time."

He glanced at Lydia as he said that, and her eyes narrowed. Money and poker… Was Jeremy gambling? It hadn't been a vice of his when they were married, but both of them had changed plenty over the years.

"Tomorrow?" Tyler pushed his glasses up his nose again. He was sweating, Lydia realized. "Yeah, okay, I can do that. Thanks, man. I really appreciate it. I'll pay you back, I swear."

"I didn't agree to give you money," Jeremy muttered, but Tyler was already hurrying away, and he ended the sentence with a sigh.

"I have questions, but first things first. I can't take your shift tonight."

"Why not?" he asked, turning to face her more fully and crossing his arms. "I know it'll be a long day for you, but I'm willing to work the first half of it, so you'll get a break, and you'll have the whole weekend off instead of just Saturday in exchange."

"Because I have plans of my own tonight," she snapped. "I'm going to dinner and a movie with a friend, and I don't feel like canceling it just so you can go on a date. I'm happy for you and Melanie, but I have my own life to live."

He blinked at her. "You're dating someone?"

He looked so shocked at the idea that she felt a little insulted. "Not that it's any of your business, but no. We're going as friends. I do have a life of my own, Jeremy. I'm not going to drop everything because you're bad at planning."

He frowned. "Sorry. I didn't think you'd have anything going on."

"Do you think I just sit around at home all day when I'm not here?"

He shrugged and looked uncomfortable, which was as close to admitting it as he was going to get. She pressed her lips together but refrained from saying anything else about it. If Jeremy thought she was some boring old spinster, it wasn't *her* problem. And in all fairness, he wouldn't have been too far off the mark a year ago.

Instead, she focused on her newest concern. "Who was that man? You're not gambling, are you? I don't care what you do with your own money, but if you do something to jeopardize the restaurant —"

"I'd never do that," he said quickly. "I play online poker sometimes; it's not a big deal. Tyler's a friend. I got him into it, but he doesn't know when to quit. I'm not the one with the problem."

"Fine," she said, crossing her arms.

"I'll figure something else out for tonight," he told her. "Have a good time at your ... movie."

He left, giving her an odd, considering look on his way out. She glared at him until the restaurant's door shut behind him.

She had worked hard to have more to her life than work, and she felt so much happier now that she was seeing her friends more and had hobbies outside of cooking. Jeremy had no right to look as shocked as he did when he learned she had plans.

TWO

Her evening out with Jude was perfect, and she was glad she hadn't canceled it so Jeremy could go on his date. What she *did* regret was not being brave enough to take the chance to kiss Jude goodbye when they parted ways for the night. She had been truthful when she told Jeremy it wasn't a date, but what she hadn't mentioned was the fact that she wished it was.

For the past couple of months, it felt like she and Jude were walking on a balance beam between being just friends and being something more. She wasn't blind; she knew when he was flirting with her, and she knew there was a spark between them, but neither of them had made the leap yet. She had been on the verge of just asking him on a date herself a couple of weeks ago, but the time hadn't been right, and then the restaurant started getting more and more popular and she had been too busy to think on it very much.

Maybe she was just using her busy work life as an excuse. As she drank her coffee the next morning and watched the squirrels squabble under the bird feeder on the lawn across the street, she wondered if she wasn't *busy* so much as she was a complete and utter coward.

"*Jeremy* has no problem asking people out on dates," she muttered. "I'm going to do it. The next time I see Jude, I'll ask him out to dinner, and I'll make it clear it's a date. I don't have to wait around for him to ask me."

Neither the squirrels across the street nor her coffee mug replied to her, but that was fine. It was a promise to herself; she was the only one who needed to witness it.

She spent a productive morning at home, going through her closet to move her cold weather clothing to the back and bring her warmer weather clothes to the forefront. Spring was in full swing now, and the season for sweaters was past.

When she drove in to work that afternoon, she kept her vehicle's windows cracked. The fresh air was energizing and seemed full of promise.

When she arrived at work, Jaelin waved her over to the hostess' station before she could go into the kitchen. A little concerned — she didn't know what Jaelin might need to talk to her about that she couldn't go to Jeremy for, and he had the morning shift today—she joined her employee behind the hostess' station and waited until Jaelin was done helping the guest she was with.

"What's up?" she asked in the lull between customers.

"Some lady came in about an hour ago asking if you were here," Jaelin said, getting right to the point. "She was very specific that she only wanted to talk to you, and it seemed important. I told her you'd be in this evening and offered to take a message for her, or jot down her number so you could give her a call, but she was insistent on speaking to you in person. I wanted to give you a heads-up; she said she'd come back around five."

Lydia frowned, racking her brain as she tried to figure out who might want to talk to her so badly. "What was her name?"

"She didn't say. Sorry, I should have asked, but it was in the middle of the lunch rush, and there was a line behind her. She didn't say what it was about, either."

"Huh. I guess just send someone to get me if she comes back. You can have her wait at the bar, and tell her I'll be out to see her as soon as I get a chance."

She was still puzzling over the mystery as she entered the kitchen, though she didn't have long to dwell on it. As soon as she put her purse down, tied her apron on, and finished washing her hands, Jeremy came over in a hurry, taking his own apron off and tossing his chef's hat toward the shelves set aside for their personal belongings.

"I rescheduled the date with Melanie for tonight, so I'm out of here," he said. "You've got one big order in the queue, might want to get started on that first. That one burner is acting up again; keep it under two or it kicks the heat all the way up to high."

He left before she could get a word out, and she wrinkled her nose at his back as the swinging door closed behind him, blocking him from her sight. She suspected he had purposefully left the big order for her to do, since he was in such a hurry to get out of here.

Sighing, she went over to the front of the kitchen to snag the order tag and see what all she had to do, then called hellos to her employees as she went over to the fridge to begin selecting the right cuts of meat.

It was shaping up to be another busy shift. She wasn't complaining; the boost in business was only good for the restaurant, but she would be lying to herself if she said a part of her didn't miss the quieter days, when she had time to breathe between orders.

The time flew by as she made one order after another. Mira, their new junior chef, was still getting used to where everything was in the kitchen and hadn't quite picked up the rhythm that the long-term employees had, but she was still a big help.

Lydia had taken a liking to her right away and was glad that Jeremy had agreed she was the best candidate after they finished their round of interviews. She was young, in her early twenties and fresh out of culinary school, but she was clearly passionate about cooking. Lydia knew Mira would be hard pressed to find another opportunity like the one they were offering her, at least not without moving hours away. Between her and Chartreuse, the sous chef that was working with Lydia today, they could handle everything Lydia didn't have the time to do.

It also meant that, when Gabe, their other new server, came into the kitchen and approached her with an expression that said he was unsure if he should interrupt her but felt like he needed to, and told her that Jaelin had sent him back to tell her that the mystery woman was back and was waiting at the bar for her, she could let her sous chef and junior chef handle the cooking for a few minutes while she went to see what this was all about.

She was half expecting to find a saleswoman waiting for her; they came in sometimes to try to sell appliances or knife sets, though Quarry Creek being so out of the way helped keep their numbers down. But the woman who was sitting at the end of the bar in a sweater dress and leggings, nervously fiddling with a glass of water before reaching up to smooth a hand over her strawberry blonde hair, did not look like a saleswoman.

Her appearance gave no other hints about what she was there for, though, so Lydia approached her from the side, a polite but guarded smile on her face.

"Hello," she said, the word making the woman snap her head over to look at her. She seemed jumpy and nervous, which put Lydia on edge. "I'm Lydia Thackery, head chef and part-owner of Iron and Flame. Are you the one who wanted to speak with me?"

"Yes." The woman set her glass of water down and smoothed a shaking hand over the front of her sweater dress. She looked to be about Lydia's age, maybe a little older judging by the faint crow's feet at the corners of her eyes. Now that she was closer, Lydia could see a few strands of grey in her hair. "I'm Marcy Calhoun."

That was nice, but it didn't tell Lydia anything about what she wanted. "How can I help you?"

Marcy took a deep breath. "I'm your sister."

Lydia stared at her. The words made sense—she understood each of them individually—but the sentence didn't. Her mind felt like it was short circuiting; not like a scratched record, but like a record player where someone had removed the record altogether, leaving only sudden silence and the crackle of the speakers.

"No, you're not."

The denial came out of her mouth seemingly of its own accord. She *had* a sister already, and this woman wasn't her.

"Well, half-sister," Marcy amended. "I know it probably comes as a surprise. I was hoping we could talk —"

The restaurant's front door opened. Lydia glanced toward it reflexively, noting the woman who came in with her phone pressed to her ear before she looked back at Marcy. There was no way. She didn't have a half-sister.

Did she?

She opened her mouth to say ... *something*, she wasn't sure what, but noticed Marcy was still staring at the woman who had come in. The woman had marched right past Jaelin's station and was standing about fifteen feet away from the bar where Lydia and Marcy were talking, and her eyes were fixed on

Marcy with an expression of pure hatred as she spoke into her phone.

"Yes, she's here. I knew I recognized her car. Please, send someone right away. This woman killed my fiancé. You need to arrest her."

THREE

The newcomer's words were loud enough that everyone seated at the surrounding tables heard what she said, and the effect was instantaneous. The low hum of conversation turned into a louder babble in an instant, and all attention quickly focused on Marcy.

Marcy was pale. She leaned back on her stool, as if to put more space between herself and the woman who was still glaring daggers at her, and her elbow bumped her water glass, knocking it over and sending water and ice spilling across the bar. No one moved to clean it up; even Lydia's employees were too shocked to do anything but stare.

Lydia realized with a jolt that she needed to do something. She was the boss, she had to be the responsible one, no matter how shocked and confused she was.

"Everyone, please calm down," she said, raising her voice slightly so her guests could hear her over the noise. "Gabe, bring some paper towels over here. Miss... Marcy, right? Please stay where you are. And you, ma'am," she said, directing her words to the woman who was on the phone. "Are you speaking to the authorities?"

The woman gave a sharp nod. "The police are on their way. You'd better stay put; they aren't going to be happy if they have to chase you down." She directed the last sentence toward Marcy, who pressed a hand to her chest as if saying, *me?*

"I didn't do anything, though," she said, her tone full of puzzlement. "You must have me mistaken for someone else."

"You're staying at the Six Pines Motel, you drive a silver hatchback, and you're a good-for-nothing homewrecker who murdered my fiancé when you realized he would never leave me for you!"

The woman took a step forward, but the dispatcher on the phone must have said something because she paused and took a slow breath in before refocusing her attention on the call.

"Right, sorry," she muttered. "My name? Nellie Long. Yes, I can give a statement…"

She retreated a few steps and lowered her voice as she continued to speak to the dispatcher. In the distance, Lydia heard sirens. Marcy jolted, drawing Lydia's attention back to her as the other woman reached for her purse.

"What are you doing?"

"I don't know what's going on, but I didn't do anything," Marcy said. "That woman's crazy. Look, can I leave you my number? I'd really like to talk to you. You can call me anytime. I took the week off work to do this, so I'll be in town until next Friday."

"Hold on, I think you should stay," Lydia said. "The police are going to want to talk to you."

"But I didn't do anything!"

"They're still going to want to talk to you. If you really didn't do whatever that woman accused you of, then I'm sure they'll get it straightened out quickly." She paused. "And it will probably look better if you stay and talk to them instead of leaving."

Marcy's brows pulled together slightly, and Lydia wondered if she was imagining how much the other woman looked like Lillian when she did that. No, there was no way she had a sister she didn't know about. It was impossible.

"You're probably right," Marcy admitted after a moment. "I'm sure this will get straightened out in no time at all."

What followed was an awkward minute or two, though it felt much longer, while Marcy fidgeted, Nellie glared, and Lydia tried to mentally sort through the roller coaster of the last few minutes, all while the sirens drew closer and the guests stared at them. A few people were recording the whole thing on their phones.

Finally, the door to the restaurant opened, and a uniformed officer came in. Lydia stepped back, listening as he talked to both Nellie and Marcy, then asked Marcy to accompany him to the station. As she followed him out, Marcy looked over her shoulder to Lydia, her gaze frightened and imploring. She knew in her gut she hadn't seen the last of this woman who claimed to be her half-sister, and she was too shaken to even begin to process everything that had just happened.

Nellie followed the officer out too, and just like that, the day's distraction ended, and her guests all went back to their meals, though the buzz of conversation remained a bit louder than usual. From the other side of the restaurant, Jaelin gave Lydia a *I can't believe that just happened* look, and Lydia returned it with a matching look of her own.

She had expected today to be busy. She hadn't expected it to be completely and utterly insane.

The entire fiasco took longer than she expected, and she felt guilty about asking Mira and Chartreuse to keep covering for her for another few minutes when she walked back into the kitchen, but Marcy's claim had gotten to her. She had to know.

She wasn't prepared to call her parents yet—there was no way *that* would be a short conversation—but Lillian might have some advice for her. At the very least, once she told Lillian what had happened, she wouldn't have to suffer through this confusion and uncertainty alone.

Lillian, her younger sister by two years, worked as a paralegal for a local law firm. Lydia knew she was still at work, but this was important enough that it was worth an interruption to her sister's day, so when her first call went through to voicemail, she tried again right after; the universal sign that this call was *important*.

Her sister answered on the third ring this time, her words brusque but laced with concern. "Lydia? What's going on?"

She hesitated, because she hadn't planned what to say in advance. Whatever words she chose, she knew they would sound crazy. She decided to just get to the point. They were both supposed to be working, and as important as this was, their jobs wouldn't wait for them forever.

"A woman just visited me at work claiming to be our half-sister," she said. "I didn't get a chance to talk with her for long—I'll tell you more about that later —but I don't know what to think. Mom and Dad never said anything to you...?"

Lillian was silent for a moment, probably processing her words. Lydia didn't blame her; it was a lot to take in.

"No, never. It's probably a scam. I bet she's going to ask you for money. You know Dad, he would never have an affair."

"Yeah." Her father was one of the best people she knew. Both her parents were. ——She didn't see them as much anymore—they had retired out of state and her mother didn't fly well, and it was hard for Lydia to get enough time off work to go visit them—but she loved them and had always thought the world of them. She would never suspect either of them of infidelity. But… "She had strawberry blonde hair. Not red, like ours, but close. And maybe it was just my mind playing tricks on me, but I think she looked a little like us. She had my nose, and your facial expressions."

"Did you think that before she claimed to be related to us, or after?"

Lydia frowned. "After, I guess." She felt something relax in her chest. Maybe her entire worldview wasn't about to be shaken after all. "I'm sure you're right. It's probably some sort of scam. I'll let you know if she contacts me again."

"And I'll let you know if she tries me next," Lillian promised. "Are you going to call Mom and Dad?"

"I think I'm going to wait and see what happens. I don't want to start a big to-do if she really is some scammer trying to make a quick buck."

She and Lillian ended the call with a few words of goodbye between them, and a promise to talk more later. Lydia didn't have much time to dwell on it after that and dove back into work with a renewed focus that came from determinedly ignoring all of the other distractions in her life.

It wasn't until close, while she was waiting for Jaelin to walk Gabe through the cashing out process so he could get his tips, that Chartreuse, who had lingered to show Mira a few tips and tricks around the kitchen, made a soft noise of surprise while she stared at her phone screen and reminded Lydia of the other thing that had happened today. The murder accusation.

"You guys, someone was killed at that old motel just outside of town. It happened earlier today."

Jaelin looked up from the cash register with a frown, her eyes meeting Lydia's. "You don't think that's what the woman from earlier was talking about, do you?"

"It has to be," Lydia said, taking her own phone out of her pocket to pull up a webpage so she could check the local news herself. "Did the article say if the police arrested anyone?"

They hadn't. There was very little news on the murder, in fact. The article she found reported it in just a few, barebones sentences and warned the people of Quarry Creek to be on their guard. It ended by urging the reader to call the number listed below if they had any information on the crime. It didn't say who had been murdered, though it indicated that the victim was male, and it certainly didn't go into any helpful details such as what the murder weapon was or who the suspects were. It didn't say anything about Marcy being arrested, and since the article had been published *after* the police brought her in for questioning, she figured that meant they had let her go.

She didn't know whether that was a good thing or not. Either the police had let her go because she was innocent, or they had let her go because she *convinced* them she was innocent, despite her guilt. The last thing Lydia wanted to deal with was a crazy person who not only claimed to be her half-sister, but was also a murderer. That would raise the stakes of Marcy's scam from moderately annoying to potentially deadly.

Maybe the police scrutiny would spook Marcy, and she would give up on whatever game she was playing and go home. Even though Lydia hoped for that outcome, her gut told her she hadn't seen the last of Marcy Calhoun.

FOUR

Even though she was all but convinced that Marcy was lying about being related to her, Lydia fell asleep that night feeling like she was clutching a dirty secret to her chest, and the feeling lingered into the morning. She *thought* Marcy was lying, but the seed of doubt had been planted, and no matter what she told herself, she couldn't stop it from taking root.

"There is no way I have a half-sister no one knows about," she told the potted plant above her sink. "That's just crazy. She's some scammer who thinks she can get money out of me, or maybe she was hoping I would help protect her from the murder accusation. Whatever the truth is, she is not my sister."

The pothos hung there silently, its green leaves too cheerful for her mood. She watered it with a glare, though she fully knew she was being ridiculous. Talking to a houseplant was a new low, but with the nice spring weather, Jude had started bringing Saffron to work with him more often than not, safe in the knowledge that she wouldn't get too cold if she had to wait in the cab of his truck. The days he was going to be out and about for most of his shift he still brought her over, and Lydia enjoyed spending her free hours before or after work with the friendly yellow dog.

A few of Saffron's belongings had permanently found their way into her house, and Jude always apologized for using her as a glorified dog sitter, but she didn't mind. She enjoyed the company. Saffron might not be a better conversationalist than her potted plant, but she was a *much* better companion.

Today was Saturday, though, which meant no work for Jude and no work for her. She only had the one day off this weekend—a part of her wished she had taken up Jeremy's offer and traded shifts with him so she could have Sunday off too—and she knew all the relaxation she had hoped to enjoy wasn't going to happen. Her stomach was twisted into knots. She couldn't stop thinking about Marcy.

As if her thoughts had summoned the woman, her phone dinged with the new notification. She picked it up and stared at the new friend request from her social media app.

She was equal parts tempted to accept it and to delete it, so she ended up ignoring it. Even without accepting the friend request, she realized Marcy's profile could be a treasure trove of information. She clicked on the woman's name and followed the link to her *About* section. It looked like a real profile, which was one mark against the theory that Marcy was working on a scam. The profile was six years old, had just over a hundred friends, and all of the pictures Lydia could see were normal pictures of Marcy living her life.

Lydia learned that Marcy lived in Chicago. Chicago was where her father had gone to graduate school. It was where he met her mother. Had he also met someone else there?

Marcy was divorced. She had one child, a boy who, according to the posts on her profile, had gone away to his first semester of college this spring. She had a pet cat. She worked in the insurance industry.

She was completely average. That, more than anything, made Lydia wonder if she and Lillian were wrong. If this was somehow *real*. There was no sob story here, no fake profile to keep her scam victims away from her real life, no indication that Marcy was anyone other than exactly who she said she was.

But Marcy hadn't only claimed to be Lydia's half-sister. She had also been accused of murder and was taken away by the police right in front of Lydia's eyes. That wasn't *normal*. That was about as far from normal as she could get. Maybe Marcy had secrets that she didn't share on her social media profile.

Hungry for more information, she navigated to a local news page and started searching for updates about the murder at the motel from yesterday. There was one article that had been published only half an hour ago, and she clicked on it eagerly.

Thankfully, this article was less bare bones than the one she had read yesterday. It still didn't give a cause of death, and there was no update about any arrests, but it gave her a name. The victim was Robert Black. He was from out of town and had been found dead in his hotel room about two hours before Lydia spoke with Marcy.

There was even a picture of him; he was a middle-aged man, just beginning to bald, with a bright grin. In the photo, he was seated at a card table, proudly holding up a hand of four aces. He looked happy. Normal. She might not have known him, but she still felt sick at the thought that he was dead now, and slowly clicked out of the article.

Had Marcy done that? Had she murdered him? Lydia had no idea what to believe, and she wished Marcy had never shown up yesterday to plunge her into this mess.

Robert Black. Why did that name sound familiar? Not his surname, but the name *Robert* rang a bell somewhere in her mind. It wasn't exactly an uncommon name, but she knew this wasn't the Robert who bagged her groceries at the store. Was he a guest at the restaurant? Someone one of her employees or Jeremy had mentioned?

The thought of her ex-husband reminded her of that nervous man, Tyler, who had ambushed him when he was trying to flee the scene after attempting to shove his evening shift off onto her. All of a sudden, she knew why the name seemed so familiar, and why the fact that he had been murdered in a motel was bothering her.

"Robert's serious about it, I don't think he's going to leave me alone until I pay up. I have until Sunday to get him the money, that's when he goes back home. I'm in real trouble if I don't have it by then."

That was what Tyler told Jeremy. It had raised red flags in Lydia's mind at the time, because she was worried that if Jeremy was getting into gambling, it could lead to him putting his stake in the restaurant on the line. Now, it raised red flags for another reason entirely.

A man named Robert was in town to collect money. If he was going home on Sunday, that meant he was a visitor, and where did visitors stay? The motel was the obvious answer.

She reopened the webpage to look at the picture of Robert in the article again, her eyes fixed on the playing cards. Jeremy said he had gotten Tyler into playing poker online, and Robert certainly looked like someone who enjoyed playing poker. There was a link here, she was almost sure of it. If Robert was involved in the seedier side of the gambling world, if he had lent money to a man who couldn't pay it back, then maybe Marcy really *hadn't* killed him.

Even if Marcy was lying about being related to Lydia, it didn't mean she was lying about not being a murderer. Scammer or not, she didn't deserve to face trouble for a serious crime she hadn't committed.

She wanted to know more, but Jeremy would be opening the restaurant right now, and she wasn't sure if she wanted to tell him about Marcy anyway. He would hear about the police being called on her from the employees, but no one had witnessed Marcy claiming to be her sister. That wasn't the sort of thing they shared anymore. Without knowing *why*, though, he might be reluctant to tell her more about Tyler and why he needed that money.

She would have to think about what to tell Jeremy. For now, there was someone else who she actually wanted to confide in, someone she knew she could rely on. Someone who could look at the entire situation with a little more distance than she and Lillian had.

She hoped Jude was up for a hike today. It would be nice to see Saffron too. The pair of them never failed to cheer her up, and she could use a little cheer.

FIVE

Jude was happy to meet her for a hike and picked her up shortly after noon. Saffron sat between them on the bench seat in the cab of his truck, her lopsided ears pricked forward eagerly as she gazed out through the windshield. Lydia ran her fingers through the dog's fur idly, making Saffron thump her tail against her thigh.

"Did you end up getting the whole weekend off anyway?" Jude asked as he navigated the familiar streets to their favorite trailhead.

"No," she said. She had told him about Jeremy's attempt to trade shifts. They hadn't been planning on getting together this weekend, since she wanted to use her one day off to get some chores and errands done and then relax, but circumstances had changed. "I just needed to get out of the house and get your opinion on something. I figured this way I could kill two birds with one stone."

He raised his eyebrows, though he kept his eyes on the road. "What's going on?"

"Let's talk about it once we're on the trail. It's ... a little crazy."

She could tell he was dying of curiosity, but he didn't press her, and by then, they were only a couple of minutes away from the small parking lot at the trailhead. As soon as they pulled in and Saffron recognized where they were, her tail started wagging like crazy, and she let out an eager, high-pitched bark that sounded like it should have come from a much smaller dog.

Lydia took Saffron's leash and got out of the truck, glad for the distraction of walking the dog. By now, Saffron listened to her almost as well as she listened to Jude, and Jude seemed to like the interest she took in walking and playing with his dog. He gave her a brief grin, stooped to scratch Saffron's ears, then gestured toward the trailhead.

"Couldn't have asked for a better day," he said. "Lead the way."

They set off down the trail, Saffron leading the way. It *was* a gorgeous day, warm and sunny with a slight breeze that ruffled the new leaves. It was late spring, nearly summer, but still early enough that the forest had a fresh feel to it.

She gathered her thoughts as they walked, then finally said, "Something happened yesterday. I'm still not sure what to think, but it really shook me. Lillian thinks it's a scam, and I know it probably is, but there's a part of me that can't stop thinking ... what if it's not?"

"What happened, Lydia?"

"Someone came into the restaurant looking for me. A woman. She claimed to be my half-sister ... and about thirty seconds later, someone else came in and accused her of murder. She was taken away by the police about five minutes later."

He let out a low whistle. "I don't know what I was expecting, but it wasn't that. Your sister thinks this woman was trying to scam you?"

"I called her while I was at work, just in case she somehow knew something I didn't. I still need to talk to her about it more, but that was her gut reaction."

"Not yours, though."

"No," she admitted. "I'm not saying I think she's related to me, but she seemed sincere. Maybe ... maybe she's mistaken. Maybe she has the wrong person."

"Well, you could always do a DNA test to be sure," he said. "It might take a few weeks, but at least that way, you'll know. Have you talked to your parents yet?"

"I haven't. I've been putting it off, to be honest. I don't think my dad would ever be unfaithful, but I guess there's a part of me that's afraid to find out. And I don't see how my mom could have a secret kid."

"Well, how old is she? Is it possible she was conceived before your parents were together?"

She frowned. She hadn't thought of that. Her parents had dated for two years before getting married, and had her nearly a year after their wedding, which meant Marcy would have to be a minimum of three years older than her. She thought of the faint grey strands in the other woman's hair and the crow's feet around her eyes. She certainly didn't seem *younger* than Lydia.

"It's possible," she admitted.

A little of her stress eased. She really hadn't wanted to learn a dark secret about one of her parents. If Marcy really was related to her, and Jude's theory was correct, then no one had been unfaithful. They had just somehow ... not known about Marcy.

She shook her head. She was getting ahead of herself. She still didn't know whether or not Marcy was telling the truth.

"Putting the question of whether we're related aside for a moment, I'm also concerned that she or Jeremy might be involved in that murder that happened at Six Pines Motel yesterday..."

She told him about Nellie, the woman who followed Marcy into the restaurant to accuse her of murdering her fiancé, then she told him what little she had found out about the victim and why she thought he might have something to do with one of Jeremy's friends.

"And don't get me started on the fact that Jeremy has been gambling. Even if he's just playing poker for fun and doesn't put a significant amount of money into it, it still makes me worried. He owns a stake in Iron and Flame. If he develops a gambling problem, he could put the entire restaurant at risk."

"I'm not saying that's not important, but the homicide is probably the more urgent matter to focus on," he said. "I heard about the murder, though only briefly. The police haven't made any arrests yet, have they?"

"Not that I know of. But you and I both know that doesn't guarantee Marcy is innocent. They might not have had enough to hold her on, even if they suspect she's behind it."

"No, but it means that she's not sitting in a jail cell. She's somewhere we can talk to her. Or you can, if you want to do it alone."

"Do you think I should?" she asked. If Marcy was involved in the murder, or even if she was simply a scammer trying to get something from Lydia, avoiding her seemed like the most sensible option.

"I do. Send her a message online, or track down her phone number and call her. See if she'll agree to doing a DNA test. Ask her about whatever happened at the motel. You don't even know for sure that she's staying there or whether she knew the victim—the woman who accused her might not know what she's talking about. You also aren't certain that the man who died is the same Robert who Jeremy's friend was talking about."

"That's true. Maybe I'm getting ahead of myself."

"There's a lot going on," he said gently. "I don't doubt that, but if there's one thing humans are good at, it's seeing connections and patterns where there aren't necessarily any. I think you need to get the full story and a clearer view of everything that's happening before you can come to any conclusions. I'm not saying that you should trust this woman completely, but you said it yourself. You're always going to wonder about it if you don't at least try to figure out the truth. Even if it is some sort of scam like your sister thinks, she can't harm you if you're careful. Don't give her money or any personal information. Don't believe anything without proof ... but I do think you should try to figure out if that proof exists."

She took a deep breath, inhaling the warm spring air. It smelled like green, growing things, and left her with a hopeful feeling in her chest. Jude was right. She didn't know enough about Marcy or the murder to be sure of anything. Sitting around and worrying about it wouldn't get her the answers she needed. Being proactive and reaching out would.

When they reached the midpoint of the path at the top of the hill, Lydia sat on a fallen log, taking a short break while Jude poured some bottled water into his cupped hand so Saffron could have a drink. She pulled out her phone and brought up Marcy's social media page. Before she could talk herself out of it, she sent the woman a brief message, to the point but polite.

Hey there, this is Lydia from Iron and Flame. I've been thinking about yesterday's conversation, and I would like to know more. If you're available, message me back, and we can figure out a time to meet. I'm free all day, starting in about an hour.

She hoped Marcy didn't keep her waiting long. She wanted answers.

SIX

She and Jude finished their hike; a three-mile loop that led to the top of one of the largest hills in the Wisconsin State Forest near Quarry Creek, then back down, where it rejoined the path to the parking lot. They didn't see anyone else on their hike, which wasn't an unusual occurrence and was one of the reasons they loved this particular trail so much.

The elevation gain was killer on her legs, but it also meant the trail wasn't usually crowded. They could put Saffron on a long leash and let her roam ahead while they chatted, taking up the whole trail if they wanted, without having to move to the side to let other groups pass by. The hike always left her feeling pleasantly tired—not exhausted, but with a burn in her muscles that told her she had completed some worthwhile exercise and left her feeling relaxed for the rest of the day. Today was no exception, and by the time they reached Jude's truck in the parking lot, she was feeling a lot less anxious and a lot more curious about what was to come.

There was even a small part of her that hoped Marcy was telling the truth. She tried to ignore it, tried to keep her expectations under control, but she couldn't deny that it was there. A new sister, a new family member to get to know. The thought was a little exciting, even if it was daunting. There was a long road between all this uncertainty and knowing the truth, though. Weeks at the minimum, depending on if Marcy was willing to do a DNA test or not. If she wasn't, well, Lydia supposed that would answer the question for her.

Her cell service was spotty on the trail, but almost as soon as they reached the truck, her phone buzzed with an incoming message. She scrambled to check it, hoping it was Marcy, and she wasn't disappointed.

I was so glad to see your message. I was certain I had messed everything up. Getting escorted out of the restaurant by the police was so embarrassing. Before you ask, I didn't have anything to do with killing anybody. I don't know what that woman was thinking. I definitely want to meet up. I'm staying at the Six Pines Motel, and I'm not familiar with the town. Would you be comfortable coming to my room? If not, is there a coffee shop or somewhere else you can recommend? After what happened at your restaurant, I don't blame you at all if you want to meet somewhere public!

She delayed answering the message long enough to help Jude wipe the mud off of Saffron's paws and load the dog into the truck, then got in herself. As soon as she buckled her seatbelt, she started tapping on her phone's keyboard. She was about to ask if Marcy wanted to meet at the Morning Dove Café, but she paused before finishing the response.

Meeting at the café would be the safer option, there was no question about that, but going to the motel might help her get answers to her questions about the murder. Even if Marcy was telling the truth and she wasn't involved in Robert's death, the connection to Jeremy still had her worried. The confirmation that Marcy was staying at the Six Pines Motel was alarming, but the fact that the woman was offering to meet her somewhere public soothed her worries a little.

"Is that her?" Jude asked as he buckled his own seatbelt and started the truck.

"Yeah. She's offering to meet me either at the motel or somewhere public. I'm tempted to meet her at the motel, but I don't want to go alone. I hate to ask, but would you be willing to drive me there and keep an eye on things from the parking lot, so I have some backup in case something happens? I feel like I should talk to her alone. If she *is* telling the truth, then this is probably a very personal matter for her."

"You don't have to ask me twice," he said. "We'll be happy to be your backup, won't we, Saffron?"

At the sound of her name, the dog wagged her tail. She was panting happily, and looked eager for another adventure, despite the three-mile walk they had just gone on.

Lydia smiled. "Thanks. If you're hungry, put a takeout order in at Iron and Flame while you're waiting, and we can pick it up for lunch afterward. My treat—I owe you and Saffron for playing the role of backup today."

"You hear that, girl? We're getting paid and everything. I should quit my job and go into the private sector."

The dog seemed overjoyed at the idea, her entire body wiggling as Jude scratched his fingers through the thick fur on her neck and ruffled her lopsided ears. She retaliated by trying to lick his face. The front seat of the truck wasn't the best place for them to roughhouse, and Lydia had to fend off the dog's tail as she responded to the message.

I'd be happy to meet at your motel. What room are you in? I can be there in about 10 minutes.

Marcy responded in an instant. *Room 4. I'm so excited to talk to you some more. See you soon!*

Jude drove them to the motel, which was a few miles down the state highway outside of town. Lydia had never stayed there, though she had driven past the turn-in for it a thousand times. As Jude pulled into the parking lot and parked in front of Room 4, next to a silver minivan that had a tag from a car rental company on the back, Lydia wrinkled her nose.

"This place looks like it's straight out of a horror movie. How are they still in business?"

Room 12, at the far end of the building, had a board over its windows, and Room 2 had crime scene tape across its door. There were weeds growing from the cracks in the parking lot, and a handful of shingles were missing from the roof. What grass there was, was overgrown, and there were bits of trash and debris on the walkway in front of the doors to the rooms. The place looked more than rundown; it looked like it was on the verge of being condemned.

"Because the only other options are that bed and breakfast in town, which charges an arm and a leg, or one of the chain hotels that's three times as far from Quarry Creek as this place is," Jude pointed out.

"Well, if you hear any screams, I'm counting on you to come to my rescue. I was feeling a lot more confident before I saw this place."

Jude rolled down the truck's windows halfway, and as Lydia got out of the car, Saffron took her seat, sticking her head through the passenger side window.

"Both our ears and eyes are peeled," he said. "If I hear or see anything alarming, I'll come get you. And if things are awkward and you need an excuse to leave, send me a text message, and I'll call you or come knock on the door. And if you've changed your mind and you want me to come with you, just say the word."

She shook her head, though she was still trying to gather up the dregs of her courage. "I think I should talk to her by myself. Thanks, though. I'll try not to take too long."

She wasn't ready, but she walked up to the door belonging to Room 4 anyway and knocked.

SEVEN

Marcy opened the door almost as soon as her knuckles touched it. She was wearing black slacks and a wine-red blouse, and her hair was pulled back into a loose ponytail. She had made an obvious effort to dress nicely both times Lydia saw her, which told Lydia she wanted to make a good impression. Marcy gave her a tight smile that seemed to be a perfect reflection of the nerves Lydia was feeling.

"Come on in and take a seat. I don't have any refreshments to offer you unless you're in the mood for some potato chips I picked up at a gas station in town."

"Thanks," Lydia said. "I'm fine, though."

She stepped into the motel room and looked around. It was every bit as bad on the inside as she would expect after having seen the outside. Maybe even worse. The stains on the ceiling spoke of water damage, and she was almost certain that the black substance she saw in the corner, growing through the aged wallpaper, was mold. The room smelled like stale cigarette smoke and mildew. She felt terrible for anyone who was staying here, and that included Marcy—scammer or not.

But maybe that's all part of the ploy, said a voice in Lydia's mind that sounded a lot like Lillian. She had to remind herself to keep her empathy in check. If Marcy was lying about being her half-sister, then whatever she was here for couldn't be good. Staying in what was easily the worst motel room Lydia had ever seen could be nothing more than an attempt to garner pity.

She took a seat on a rickety wooden chair near the tiny desk next to one of the two twin beds, and Marcy perched on the edge of the bed, fiddling with the hem of her blouse.

"I assume you have questions."

"So many I don't even know where to start," Lydia admitted. "Why do you think I'm your half-sister?"

"I've always known it was possible I had half siblings out there somewhere," Marcy said. "My parents met in college and had a one-night stand during a party. I was the result. My mom wasn't proud of it, but she had always wanted children and she went back home to have me with the support of my grandparents. She met the man who would become my stepfather while she was pregnant with me, and they got married not long after I was born, so she never felt the need to contact my biological father. She explained all of this to me once she thought I was old enough to understand it, so it was never a big secret."

"But you never knew who your father was?"

She shook her head. "I think she felt bad about it, because by then it was too late for her to track him down even though I was very curious about him. This was all in the eighties and the early part of the nineties, so the internet wasn't as prolific as it is now, and it wasn't as simple as looking him up on social media. All my mom knew was his first name and the college he went to, so I knew it would be a bit of a project to look him up – and it might end up leading to some complications, too, if his family wasn't happy to learn about me. I put it off for a while, but after my son, Landon, moved out to go to college, I decided it was time to finally try to figure out where I came from."

"And that led you to my father."

Marcy nodded. "I had to do some digging. It took me a while, but I managed to get a list of the students from my mom's year, and I made a list of everyone with his first name, but there were a *lot* of men named John, and she never knew his last name, so I had to talk to some of the other people she knew during her college years to have them help me connect the dots. It was hard, really hard. Finally, I met a woman who remembered that John Thackeray and Martha Durand—my mother's maiden name— were both at the same party at around the same time I was conceived. I looked him up online and showed his picture to my mom, and she confirmed it was him."

"Why did you come to me about it first, not him or my sister?" she paused.

"Lillian? Well, her online profile is set to private, and I couldn't find out where she worked or send her a message. Your profile's a little more public, and I saw that you owned that lovely restaurant, so I thought it would be easier to meet with you first. I didn't want to go straight to John in case I caused problems between him and his wife. I don't want to wreck any families or break up any marriages. My mom says they were both single when they met, but obviously, I don't know for sure if that's true or not. I'm not looking for a replacement family or a kidney or any of those horror stories you hear about sometimes, I just want to know more about where I came from and maybe get to know the people on this side of my family, if you're open to it."

Everything Marcy said seemed to line up. There was no cold, hard proof, but having heard her out, Lydia's gut told her this was real. And that changed everything. This wasn't a stranger out for her money or—like Marcy had joked about, a kidney—but rather someone who was related to her by blood. A sister she hadn't known she had.

Still, she knew she shouldn't just take Marcy's word for it. "I'm not saying I don't believe you, but would you be willing to take a DNA test to confirm that we're related?"

Marcy nodded immediately. "I figured you would ask something like that. I mean, I know I would if someone showed up claiming to be *my* sister. I'm happy to take whatever test you want. I looked a few up online, but I figured you might be more comfortable if we ordered them together."

Even though she wouldn't be completely certain until they got the results of the test back, that all but clinched it for Lydia. She exhaled in a slow sigh, then smiled at the other woman. "Well, we can order a DNA test on Monday. For now, welcome to the family."

Marcy gave her a warm smile in return. "Thanks. You don't mind, do you? I went back and forth for a long time on whether it would be better for everyone to know the truth, or if I should just leave things be."

"Speaking for myself, I'm glad you approached me. I think Lillian will feel the same, though she might be a little more difficult to convince. I'll talk to her and try to arrange something. She works as a paralegal, so she's a little more leery about this sort of thing. I think she's seen a fair number of horror stories in real life."

"That's completely understandable," Marcy said. "What about your parents? Like I said, I don't want to step on any toes, but I've been dying to know who my biological father is for years."

"Well, I'm pretty sure your mom is right that my dad was single when he met her. My parents met at the tail end of their last year of college, and my dad's not the kind of person who would lie about being in a relationship or cheat on someone. I'm guessing you're older than me?"

"Thirty-seven," Marcy said. "I'm not exactly a spring chicken anymore, but I still feel pretty young most of the time."

"I'm thirty-two," Lydia said. "Almost thirty-three. So my parents definitely weren't together when my dad and your mother met. I'm certain they would both want to know about you. Maybe we should wait until we get the DNA results back, though. It might be easier that way."

"Of course. Now that I've made contact with you and we've got a plan in the works, I'm not in a hurry at all. This is so exciting. I'm sorry if I'm coming on too strong, but I've been imagining this moment literally ever since my mom told me my stepdad wasn't my biological father. They weren't able to have any more children, and I've always wanted brothers or sisters."

"I'll give Lillian a call this afternoon, and hopefully, we can all meet up soon. In the meantime, you should get out of here," Lydia said, looking around the motel room. "There's a bed and breakfast in town. It's a little more expensive, but it doesn't have black mold on the walls."

Marcy grimaced. "I know, this place is terrible. I made the reservation over the phone, and in the pictures online, it looked all right. I've already paid for the entire week, though, and I can't afford to lose out on that money and pay for another place to stay on top of it."

Lydia's gut instinct was to offer her help to Marcy, but she had promised herself she wasn't going to put any money on the line. Even though she was relatively certain that Marcy *was* related to her, sharing blood with someone didn't mean they were a good person. Marcy could both be her half-sister and be out to scam her out of her money; the two weren't mutually exclusive. And offering a stranger a place to stay on her couch was a little too much for her peace of mind.

"Well, I'm pretty sure this place is unsafe to sleep in," she said instead. "Maybe if you complained and threatened to report the owner to whatever agency oversees motels, he'll refund you. I'm sure it would be cheaper for him than getting shut down."

Marcy hesitated, then shook her head. "I'm terrible at confrontation. I couldn't do something like that. It took me weeks to even get up the courage to come here and talk to you. Thanks for offering, though. I know the room isn't great, but it's only for a week. I'll be fine."

Lydia frowned, but she didn't know Marcy well enough to argue about it. For all that they were most likely sisters, they were still strangers. "Well, all right. If you change your mind, let me know. I'm happy to talk to the owner with you and offer whatever moral support I can. Here, let's exchange numbers."

They traded contact information, then Lydia explained that she had someone waiting for her in the parking lot. She felt a little bad about leaving so quickly, but her mind was reeling. She needed some time to let all of this sink in. She needed to talk to Lillian and let her know what was going on.

And she needed to order a DNA test as soon as possible. She didn't want there to be a single doubt left.

EIGHT

After promising to meet up with Marcy at some point tomorrow, Lydia said her goodbyes and left the motel room. She paused just outside the door and gave Jude a reassuring wave as she thought about what to do next. The motel room wasn't just ugly and gross; if it had black mold, as she suspected, then it was unhealthy. She couldn't force Marcy to demand her money back, but maybe she could raise the issue herself. If she didn't mention Marcy's name, then it shouldn't cause her any issues, right? And it might help her get out of here and spend the rest of the week somewhere better.

She gestured at Jude to give her one second, then jogged down the walkway to the office at the end of the row of rooms, just past the boarded-up room 12. She assumed Room 2, with the crime scene tape across the door, was where Robert had been murdered. She hadn't asked Marcy about it. It hadn't felt right, not after talking about their families and how vulnerable Marcy had seemed. But now she had her number, so maybe she could call her this evening and ask about what happened at the police station and if she had seen or heard anything the day Robert was killed.

She reached the motel's office and let herself inside just as another vehicle pulled into the parking lot. She hoped they weren't planning on staying here, because the more she saw, the more she became convinced that this place needed to be shut down. The interior was lit only by the sunlight that came through the windows, and it was in just as much disrepair as Marcy's motel room had been, with the unpleasant addition of the sour smell of spoiled milk.

The man behind the counter didn't even look up when she came in. He was playing a game on his cell phone with the volume turned up and seemed utterly focused on it. He was middle-aged, older than her, with close cut brown hair and a beard that looked like he had grown it out of laziness rather than any desire to have neatly groomed facial hair. She had absolutely no idea if he was the owner or an employee. He certainly wasn't wearing a name tag, and when he didn't look up even as she approached the counter, she started to wonder if he was even employed there at all.

"Excuse me?" she said trying not to sound impatient. She wasn't usually one to complain about poor service—she knew better than anyone how busy things could get in the service industry, and that just because someone was on the clock, it didn't mean they weren't having a bad day—but she wasn't feeling particularly generous toward this motel by now.

"You have a reservation?" the man grunted, still not looking up from his phone.

"No, I'm here to make a complaint. There's mold in the rooms—"

"We passed our inspection. Are you going to rent a room? If not, go bother someone else. This isn't a five-star hotel, lady. I don't want to hear this whining."

She stared at him in shock. There was laziness, and then there was blatant rudeness, and maybe she had lived too privileged a life, but she hadn't expected the latter.

"I'm sorry?" she said, managing to get past the worst of her shock. "What's your name? Does your boss know you're talking to people like that?"

"You blind or something?" he asked, finally looking up from his phone long enough to jab a finger at the wall next to the counter. "*I'm* the owner. Either pay for a room or get out of here. If I wanted to hear complaints, I'd have a complaint box on the counter."

She looked where he was pointing to see a framed photo of him and two other people, cut out from a newspaper. Under it was a plaque that read *Jacob Harris, new owner of the Six Pines Motel, on their reopening day, 2017.*

She had no idea how he had changed from the smiling man in the photo to the angry, unhappy man behind the counter, and she supposed it didn't really matter. It was clear that her hope of getting a refund for Marcy was impossible. She was glad she hadn't convinced the other woman to come confront him with her after all, and doubly glad she hadn't mentioned Marcy's name or room number.

It was obvious that asking him about the murder wasn't going to get her anywhere either. This man was unpleasant enough that she wouldn't have been surprised to learn *he* had killed Robert.

"Sorry to disturb you," she said, deciding that she wasn't going to get anywhere with him. "You have a nice day."

With that, she left the office and turned back to Jude's truck. She was looking forward to getting out of here, grabbing lunch, and relaxing somewhere normal. Just being in that motel had made her feel gross.

The car that had pulled into the parking lot as she was going into the office was parked next to Jude's truck now, but she didn't realize that the driver was on the other side of the truck, talking to Jude through the window, until she had nearly reached the vehicle.

"What's going on?" she asked, jogging the last few steps to the front of the truck so she could get a better view of whoever he was talking to.

As soon as she saw the woman's face, she realized she recognized her. Nellie Long, the woman who had accused Marcy of murder.

"She wants to talk to you," Jude called out. "I think you should hear her out."

She turned to Nellie, a silent question in her eyes.

"I don't know why you're here, but if you're involved with her somehow, you need to listen to me." Nellie crossed her arms. "I *know* that woman in Room 4 killed my fiancé. I have proof."

NINE

Lydia's eyes darted toward Marcy's room, but the curtains were drawn, and there was no peep hole in the door for her to watch out of. She had no idea Lydia was still here, let alone that the woman who had hounded her all the way to the restaurant had come back.

"She didn't—" Lydia had to cut herself off. Marcy didn't seem like a killer, but *Lydia didn't know her*. Instead of defending her, she forced herself to ask, "What proof?"

"Can we talk somewhere else?" Nellie asked. "I don't want to do this right in front of her room."

"Hold on, why are you here?" Lydia asked.

. . .

"I'm trying to get more evidence so the police will arrest her, like they should have done already," Nellie said. "I saw you coming out of her room when I pulled in, and I thought I should warn you. Do you know her? Are you her friend?"

"This is the second time I've ever spoken to her," Lydia said. She wasn't sure she wanted to reveal Marcy's claim of sisterhood, and thankfully, Nellie didn't ask her what they had been talking about.

"Well, can we talk somewhere else? I have proof, but it's not enough for the police. Maybe you can help me get more."

Lydia looked at Jude through the windshield, not wanting to inconvenience him any more than she had already done. He shrugged, easy-going as usual. "We could meet at that park in town," he suggested.

"I'm not from the area. You'll have to tell me where it is," Nellie said.

They gave her directions and, after she and Lydia had each gotten back into their respective vehicles, they left the motel's parking lot. As Jude drove away,

Lydia turned in her seat to watch Marcy's silver rental minivan slowly vanish from sight. She felt oddly guilty about going to meet up with Nellie to discuss whether or not Marcy had committed murder without talking to her first, but she had reached the point where she just wasn't sure *what* to believe.

"You doing all right?" Jude asked.

Turning around to face front, she stroked her hand down Saffron's back idly. "Yeah. It's been a crazy couple of days, that's all."

"How did your conversation with Marcy go?"

She told him about it, admitting that she believed the other woman, though she still wanted to do the DNA test. Sister or not, though, her involvement with the murder was another matter entirely. Lydia had to remember that.

Jude pulled into a parking spot near the park in Quarry Creek a few minutes later. Nellie was right behind them and took the space next to them. She waited as Lydia, Jude, and Saffron got out of the truck—Jude had offered to wait in the vehicle again, but Lydia wanted his opinion on whatever proof

Nellie had—and they walked toward the tables under one of the pavilions as a group. The park was busy, but they managed to get a table that wasn't too close to anyone else. She and Jude took one side while Nellie took the other and Saffron laid down under the table at their feet.

"Before I show you my proof, I need you to understand I don't know that woman. I have nothing against her personally. I have no reason to make this up. The first time I ever saw her was two days ago, and even given the context of what I'm about to show you... I know in my heart my fiancé was to blame, not her."

"Why exactly do you think she killed him?" Lydia asked.

She felt bad for being so blunt, but it was easy to forget that Nellie had lost someone close to her just a day ago. Even the day of the murder, when she came into Iron and Flame to accuse Marcy of murder, she had been angry but dry-eyed. Right now, she looked composed and determined, but not like she was grieving.

In response, Nellie took her cell phone out of her purse. After tapping and swiping on the screen a few times, she laid it face up on the table and slid it toward Lydia and Jude. They leaned forward to look at the image on the screen. It was grainy, as if it had been zoomed in just a little too far, but it was impossible to mistake the woman in the picture for anyone but Marcy. She was wearing the same sweater dress she'd had on yesterday, at the restaurant.

The photo showed Marcy standing outside a motel room, her hand on the door handle. At first, Lydia didn't know why this was supposed to be proof of anything, but then she saw the number on the door and realized Marcy wasn't going into her room.

She was going into Room 2.

Nellie waited long enough to be sure they had both seen it, then swiped her phone's screen, which cycled to the next picture. This one showed the door open and Marcy going inside.

When Nellie took her phone back, she looked smug. "See? It was enough to convince the police to question her, but then they let her go. I need more. Will you help me? I don't know how you know her, but if today is only the second time you've ever spoken to her, you can't know her well enough to want to help her get away with *murder.*"

"Is there a reason Marcy would be meeting your fiancé at a motel?" Jude asked. He looked skeptical—just as skeptical as Lydia felt.

Nellie's cheeks reddened. "We've been having issues for a while. I didn't want to jump right to accusing him of cheating, but he had been secretive; hiding his phone on me, talking on the phone but ending the call as soon as I came in, not letting me see his bank statement... When he said he had a business trip this weekend, I pretended to believe him, then I borrowed my sister's car and followed him. Seeing her go into his room... I wasn't surprised, just disappointed. And then, before I could confront them, she killed him. I don't know how to feel. I don't know if I should hate him for betraying me like this, or if I should feel like my heart was torn out of my chest because now, he's *dead*. I'm never going to be able to ask him why he would throw everything away for this woman, but it's not too late for me to ask *her* why she killed him."

Lydia didn't know what to say. None of this made sense with what she knew of Marcy ... but then, what did she really know about Marcy? Two conversations wasn't enough for her to know what kind of person she was.

"I don't know what to say," Lydia admitted. "I'm sorry. This is just ... a lot."

"Just promise me, if you know anything or if she tells you anything that is incriminating enough to get justice for Robert, you'll tell me. Or go straight to the police, I don't care. Here, I'll give you my phone number. Call me if you hear anything, even if it's not something you have proof of. And be careful. I don't know why she killed him. Who knows what she'll do next? That woman is crazy."

TEN

After exchanging numbers with Nellie, she and Jude said goodbye to her and drove the short distance to Iron and Flame to pick up the to-go order Jude had called in what felt like forever ago. Lydia's appetite had vanished, all the empty space in her stomach replaced by the knots of uncertainty and worry the conversation with Nellie had left behind.

She had felt like things were settled when she left Marcy's motel room. She had been optimistic. Now, she had no idea what to think.

She didn't think Marcy was lying about being her half-sister, or at least, she believed that Marcy believed it. So, how was Robert involved? Unless

Nellie was very good at doctoring photos, then it was clear Marcy *had* gone into Robert's motel room at some point. *Why?*

It was clear that she needed to talk to Marcy again, but her original plan to call her and ask about Robert's murder over the phone wasn't going to cut it anymore. There was something she was missing, and she didn't want to risk any chance of miscommunication. This was a conversation she had to have in person.

But first, she needed to talk to Lillian. It was past time she and her sister were on the same page about all of this.

She called Lillian while Jude drove them back to her house from the restaurant, the to-go bag on her lap. Saffron kept licking her lips, and Lydia narrowed her eyes and inched the bag further from the dog as the phone rang.

Occasionally, Lillian had to put hours in on the weekend, but thankfully this weekend wasn't one of them. Lydia kept the call brief, simply telling Lillian that she had spoken to Marcy and thought her claim was legitimate, and she wanted to talk about it in person. From Lillian's skeptical tone, she knew convincing her sister was going to be difficult. It was hard to keep the issue of Marcy's claim of sisterhood and her potential involvement in the murder separate. She wasn't sure yet what she was going to tell Lillian about the latter, but she was certainly going to tell her *something*. The last thing she wanted was for Lillian to seek Marcy out to talk to her without being aware that the woman might have murdered a man.

They agreed to meet at Lydia's house in an hour, which was enough time for she and Jude to eat their lunch together and talk about the emotional roller coaster that today had been.

Jude tried his best to be supportive, and Lydia appreciated it, even though it was clear he had no idea how to help her figure the entire mess out. She didn't blame him; she had no idea what to do either. Common sense told her to keep her distance from Marcy until the murder case had been solved one way or another, and to not get further involved if she could help it.

But the murder was impossible to ignore. It wasn't just Marcy who was connected, it was Jeremy's friend, Tyler. She still didn't have any proof that the Robert who died was the same Robert who Tyler mentioned, but it was too much of a coincidence. If one of Jeremy's friends was connected to the murder somehow, then it could fall back on the restaurant.

Which meant she couldn't just ignore it. If she or Jeremy were connected to the murder through Tyler or Marcy, then the restaurant's reputation might take a hit.

She didn't manage to finish her meal, but she put the leftovers in her fridge, hoping her appetite would return in time for dinner. The food was delicious, and it would be a shame to waste it.

"I'll get out of your hair and let you talk to Lillian by yourself," Jude said after they had finished tidying up the kitchen table after their meal. Saffron was lying on the rug by the front door, having passed out after drinking a whole bowl of water that Lydia put down for her. Sometimes she envied the dog its simple life.

"Wish me luck," she said. "She's already suspicious of Marcy. I don't think this is going to go well."

"Good luck," he said. "Let me know if there are any new developments with Marcy, or if you hear anything more about the murder. I'll try to do some digging and see if I can find out more about the man who was killed."

He clipped Saffron's leash to her collar and waited for Lydia to say goodbye to the dog, then let himself out the door.

Lillian arrived twenty minutes later. Just watching her sister walk up to the house, she could tell Lillian was worried.

"Please tell me you haven't signed anything or agreed to anything," she said as soon as Lydia opened the door.

"All I've done is talk to her," Lydia assured her. "Sit down. Do you want something to drink?"

"No, I want to know why you think playing into this woman's game is a good idea," Lillian said as she dropped her purse on the kitchen table and took a seat. "I've been doing research, and it's not an uncommon scam. If she can convince you not to do the DNA test, and our family accepts her as related to us, then she could have a claim to our inheritance—or maybe even to the restaurant, if something happens to you and you don't have a will in place."

"I think she's telling the truth," Lydia said, though her sister's words sent a chill up her spine. It hit too close to her fear that Marcy was involved in the murder.

"You'd better tell me what happened," Lillian said. "I can't believe you're actually giving her a chance."

Sighing, Lydia sat across from her sister and started talking. She told her all about meeting Marcy at the motel room and hearing her story. Bit by bit, Lillian's expression changed from doubtful to puzzled, and then reluctantly intrigued.

Finally, Lydia told her sister about the murder, the topic she had avoided up until now. "All I know for certain is the victim was killed two doors down from her motel room, and there is evidence that she went into his room at some point. She didn't mention anything about it, and I haven't brought it up yet."

"I'll admit that her claim sounds more realistic than I expected," Lillian said, biting her lip. "I think it might be worth it to do a DNA test if she's serious about going through with it. But there's absolutely no reason she needs to stick around for that. Ask her to give you a few strands of her hair, or make an appointment to go to a clinic and get blood drawn, then tell her to head home until we get the results back. She doesn't need to hang around town all week. And under no circumstances should you bring up your suspicions the next time you talk to her, Lydia. Who knows if she's telling the truth about anything, but if she *did* kill a man, the last thing we need is for her to think you're suspicious."

"She came all the way out here to meet us," Lydia said. "She paid for her room in advance, she took time off work... and I'm supposed to tell her to turn around and go home?"

"*Yes*," Lillian said. "And please don't give her my number or any of my contact information. If we get the DNA test back and she really is our half-sister, then I'll meet her and get to know her—assuming she isn't in prison for life by then. But I still think there's a good chance this is one big scam."

Lillian's advice was much the same as Jude's had been. Maybe they were right. Maybe she should step away from all of this and let whatever happened happen.

Or maybe she could do just a *little* more digging when she met Marcy to do the DNA test. She understood why Lillian was worried, but her sister wouldn't have to know.

ELEVEN

Lydia decided that Lillian was right about one thing, at least. Marcy didn't need to be here in Quarry Creek for the next week. If she was exactly who she said she was—a woman here to connect with family she just discovered—there was absolutely no reason for her to stay in that rundown, dirty motel room for longer than she had to. If Nellie was right and Marcy had murdered Robert, then getting her away from town would only be safer for everyone.

She did some research and found a company with good reviews that offered easy DNA tests – all they had to do was spit in the provided vial and mail it back to the company. She could overnight the packets to her house, but they still wouldn't get there until Monday, so that would have to be soon enough. She put the order in, then called Marcy to let her know.

"I thought we could get those sent out on Monday as soon as I get them, then you can go home while we wait for the results. I hate thinking about you in that motel room. Black mold is bad news."

"All right, that seems like a good idea," Marcy said, much to Lydia's relief. "I can pay you back half the cost of the tests. Just let me know how much it was, and I'll bring cash the next time we meet. Do you still want to get together tomorrow? I thought we could grab lunch."

"Unfortunately, I'm not sure if I'll have time." She felt bad for changing their plans, but Lillian's excess of caution had gotten to her. Besides, she did have to work. It was a convenient excuse. "I'll call you as soon as the tests get here on Monday."

"Sure, that works," Marcy said. She sounded slightly hurt, and Lydia hoped she would understand. If everything was as it seemed to be, they would have time to talk and bond in the future. Right now, she didn't know what to think.

She spent the rest of the evening meal prepping for the week ahead so she would have something to eat when she wasn't at the restaurant, then trying to find out more about Robert Black online. There just wasn't much information about his case. A murder in a rundown motel in the middle of nowhere wasn't exactly big news, and if there were any updates, they hadn't been made available to the public yet.

She went to bed frustrated. When she woke up, she was glad for the distraction a weekend shift would provide, even though she had been wishing for the day off just yesterday.

The restaurant was only open for six hours on Sundays, but it was one of their busiest shifts, so she got there early to prep the kitchen. None of the new employees were there that day, so the kitchen worked like a well-oiled machine. It was nice to just focus on cooking and not worry about training anyone new, dealing with any drama, or thinking of anything except how much longer the ribeye steak she was cooking needed until it was done.

Her lovely, drama free day didn't last long. An hour after opening, Noel popped into the kitchen to tell her Jeremy had arrived, and he and Melanie had put in an order for a seared tuna appetizer he wanted out ASAP.

Asking for a rush order was a little annoying, but she liked Melanie, and she didn't mind cooking for her ex-husband and his dates as long as they were polite to her. But just as she laid the fillet of pepper encrusted tuna on the hot skillet, Jeremy came into the kitchen and started rifling through the refrigerator.

"What are you doing?" she asked, craning her neck but unable to step away from the griddle. She was well and truly annoyed by now. If he was going to come in here anyway, he could have made his own appetizer instead of sending Noel to ask her to rush the order.

Even though she was irritated, she kept most of her focus on what she was doing. The tuna took mere seconds to cook on each side, just enough to sear it and leave it raw and cool on the inside.

"Go on. The tuna is for Melanie, not me," he said, giving her a dismissive wave. "I had an idea last night for a crispy asparagus with hollandaise sauce appetizer, and I wanted to try whipping it up really quickly."

"It's the middle of a Sunday shift, Jeremy," she said as he claimed a burner at the gas stove next to her. "We're busy. Can't you experiment at home?"

"It'll only take a few minutes," he said. "Tell you what, I'll make the next few orders while I'm working on this. You can take that out to Melanie when you're done. She wanted to say hi anyway."

He probably thought he was doing her a favor. In a way, he was. She would be hard-pressed to get a break for longer than a minute or two otherwise. But she had been in the zone, flying through orders and focused on what she was doing rather than the whole mess with Marcy and Robert. This interruption couldn't have been less welcome.

Still, no arguing in the kitchen was their number one rule, so she contented herself with glaring at him as she finished the tuna appetizer. After removing it from the heat, she sliced it into thin slices and plated it before drizzling sesame oil and lemon juice over it. The appetizer finished; she carried it into the dining area to find Melanie.

Noel was kind enough to point her to Jeremy and Melanie's table, which was a small table for two in the back part of the restaurant. She made sure her expression was pleasant as she approached. Melanie hadn't done anything wrong.

"One seared tuna appetizer," she said, lowering the plate to the table in front of Melanie, who looked up from her phone with a smile.

"Oh, Lydia, thank you so much for bringing this out yourself."

"I was happy to," she said. "Jeremy said you wanted to say hi."

"I wanted to make sure we're still good. I know things have been a little strained between you and Jeremy lately. I hope that doesn't have anything to do with the fact that he and I are seeing each other again."

"Not at all," Lydia assured her. "Trust me, I'm glad the two of you are dating again. I have a lot going on, but it has nothing to do with Jeremy or the restaurant, not really. Once I know more, I'll tell you about it. For now, can I get you anything else? Jeremy has temporarily kicked me out of the kitchen, but I could grab you a drink if you want something from the bar."

"Did he say how long he was going to be? If you have time, you're welcome to join me."

"I can't drink on the clock, unfortunately, but I can grab you something and sit with you," Lydia said. "What are you in the mood for?"

"I—" Melanie broke off, her gaze flicking to something behind Lydia's shoulder. "Tyler?"

Lydia turned around. Sure enough, Jeremy's friend with the gambling addiction was standing there. He was almost unrecognizable. Instead of looking nervous and flustered, he looked like the weight of the world had been taken off his shoulders. He carried a thick envelope in one hand, and he looked between her and Melanie briefly before glancing around the dining area.

"Hi, Melanie," he said. "Hi there, Ms. Thackery. I don't think we've met formally, but I'm a friend of your ex-husband's."

"I'm aware," she said, bemused. "How can I help you?"

"Jeremy said he was going to be here. I have something for him."

"He's in the kitchen at the moment," Lydia said.

"Is that the money you owe him?" Melanie asked.

Tyler nodded, and Lydia felt a surge of concern. Why did Tyler owe Jeremy money? Had he lent it to him after all? If so, it seemed awfully soon for him to be paying it back.

"I ended up not needing it, so I wanted to get it back to him as soon as possible. Do you know how long he's going to be?"

"I don't, but I can run it back to him," Lydia offered, holding out her hand. She wanted to get to the bottom of this herself.

Tyler hesitated, but he must have decided she was trustworthy, considering that she owned the restaurant along with Jeremy. He handed the envelope over to her and with a brief nod and farewell to Melanie, he made his way out of the restaurant.

"I'm going to run this to Jeremy," Lydia told Melanie. "I'll bring you that drink when I come back."

The envelope of money felt like a burning torch in her hand. Jeremy had assured her that he wasn't gambling with any significant funds, but unless this was all ones, Tyler had borrowed a *lot* of cash from him. If Jeremy was involved with people who gambled the big bucks, how long until he got sucked into it too?

He was still fiddling with his appetizer in the kitchen, and she walked right up to the counter next to him and smacked the envelope full of cash down.

"Tyler dropped this off for you," she said. "What's going on, Jeremy? I don't care what you do on your own time, but if you have a gambling problem, you need to make sure it can't touch Iron and Flame. That includes not using the restaurant to move large amounts of cash around."

"Jeeze, Lydia," he said as he took the envelope and shoved it into his pocket. "Give a man a break, will you? I told you before, I just play poker on and off. This money isn't from gambling. I lent it to Tyler as a favor to a friend, and it turned out he didn't need it. He told me the guy he owed money to passed away unexpectedly. Would you quit being so suspicious of everything I do? I care about this restaurant as much as you do. I'm not going to jeopardize it."

She still wasn't pleased, but she couldn't do anything other than believe him. But she had realized something else. This all but confirmed the man who had been murdered was the same Robert who Tyler had mentioned on Friday. That meant Robert had been in Quarry Creek to get the money Tyler owed him.

Which meant Robert wasn't here to meet with Marcy. He wasn't having an affair.

She still had no idea why Marcy had gone into his room, but Tyler had a much stronger motive to kill Robert than Marcy, a perfect stranger to Robert did.

She didn't have any proof to take to the police, but maybe with Nellie's help and knowledge of her fiancé, she could find some.

TWELVE

After bringing Melanie her drink, Lydia made her excuses and stepped outside to take her break in the fresh air and relative privacy. She leaned against the side of the restaurant as she typed out a message to Nellie.

Hey, you asked me to let you know if I found any evidence that Marcy had something to do with Robert's death. I didn't, but I think I know who else might have had a motive. If you want to talk, I should be done at the restaurant at nine, and I can call you then.

Nellie didn't reply right away, and after a few minutes, Lydia had to go back into the kitchen. By then, Jeremy had finished his experimental appetizer. He gave her a small plate to try and brought the rest of it out to share with Melanie. It *was* good – she would never deny that he was a skilled chef—and she had a feeling it was going to make its way onto their menu this summer.

Another hour passed before she got a chance to check her phone. When she did, a message from Nellie was waiting.

I would rather talk in person. Is there a bar we could meet at?

She didn't think she would have the energy to meet Nellie at a bar after her shift, and Iron and Flame would afford them more privacy anyway, so she responded by telling the other woman to meet her at the restaurant just after nine, then put her phone away to focus on the food.

The kitchen closed at nine, but a last-minute order came in two minutes beforehand, so she didn't finish cooking until ten minutes past the hour. When she was finally finished and got a chance to wash her hands, take off her hair net and apron, and sit down for the first time in hours, she checked her phone again, wondering if Nellie was here yet.

At some point over the past couple of hours, she had messaged her back. *I don't think I'll be able to make it by nine. Closer to 9:30 or 10. Is that too late?*

Lydia would rather go home and take a bath and go to bed, but she wanted to talk to Nellie and see if she was right that it was money was the reason Robert had been killed, not infidelity. She would rest more easily if she was certain that Marcy had nothing to do with it.

She started typing, *I'll be here—*

Before she could finish the message, her phone started ringing with an incoming call, and Marcy's name came up on the screen. She frowned. They had already agreed they weren't going to get together today, and Marcy shouldn't need anything from her until tomorrow. She answered the call, pressing the phone to her ear and leaning back in her chair, raising her other hand to rub at the junction of her shoulder and neck. Yes, a hot bath sounded perfect right now.

"Hello?"

"Oh, Lydia, thank goodness you answered," Marcy said. "I couldn't remember if your restaurant closed at nine or ten. I was praying it was nine. I'm panicking, I don't know what to do."

"What's going on?"

"That horrible man who owns the motel just attacked me in the parking lot. I was walking to my room from my van, and he came out of nowhere. He grabbed my shoulders and shook me and started shouting about how he didn't appreciate me sending my friend to complain about the room. He said I'd be sorry if I made trouble over it and said something about knowing the local health and safety inspector, and it being his word against mine. I managed to get away and lock myself in my room, but I don't know what to do. I have nowhere else to go, and I'm really scared he's going to hurt me. Do you know if that bed-and-breakfast you mentioned is still open? Can you give me their number? I hate to spend the money, but I have to get out of here."

Lydia's stomach dropped. Jacob must have figured out that Lydia had been visiting Marcy when she went into the office to complain about the motel room. She had tried to keep Marcy out of it, but it hadn't worked. She had made the complaint when

Marcy said she didn't want to, and now the other woman was paying for it.

"Of course, I'll get you their number. Are you safe right now? Did he leave?"

"He tried the door, but I locked it, and after a while, he walked away. I think he was drunk." Marcy paused. "Oh my goodness, you don't think he went to get his master key, do you? I latched the little chain lock, but I don't think that will hold if he's determined to get into the room and unlocks the deadbolt."

"Do you want me to go over there and keep you company while you pack?" Lydia asked. "If he comes back, you shouldn't be alone."

"Would you? That would make me feel a lot better."

"I can be there in about ten minutes. Here, I'm going to hang up and I'll text you the number for the bed-and-breakfast. While you call them, I'll start driving over. After you've arranged a room, call me back, and I'll stay on the phone with you until I get there."

After ending the call and sending the number as promised, she quickly texted Nellie.

Sorry, something came up. Not going to be able to meet tonight, maybe we can meet in the morning.

She still desperately wanted to tell the other woman about Tyler and the money he had owed Robert, but the fear in Marcy's voice had been real. She needed her help. Tyler would have to wait. For now, Lydia was going to trust her gut, and her gut said Marcy wasn't involved with the murder.

She made sure her employees were prepared to close on their own, then hurried out to the parking lot, where she wasted no time in getting into her SUV. She wasn't the only person leaving; someone else backed out of their parking spot a moment after she did, but she didn't feel bad about hurrying to reach the parking lot's entrance before they did. If they were turning left, she didn't want to get stuck behind them.

After making her turn, she took her eyes off the road long enough to check that her phone's volume was turned up so she could hear when Marcy called.

She didn't have long to wait. As soon as her ringtone went off, she answered the call through her phone's bluetooth system.

"Are you all right?" she asked as she glanced in the rearview mirror. She wished the person behind her would pass her; they were following close, and their headlights were distracting.

"He hasn't come back yet," Marcy said. "I called the bed-and-breakfast. The woman who answered the phone was so nice. She's getting me a room tonight and said we can figure everything else out in the morning. Are you still coming to the motel?"

"Yeah, I'm on my way," Lydia said. "Put your phone on speaker and start packing. That way, if he comes back, I'll be able to hear it, and I'll call the police."

"Thanks for doing this, Lydia," Marcy said, her voice growing fainter as she followed Lydia's suggestion. "I don't know what happened; he just went crazy. I've never been so afraid in my life."

Lydia didn't blame her. Jacob had a mean side to him, that much had been obvious even from their brief conversation. She wouldn't be surprised for an instant if he seriously injured or even killed someone in the heat of the moment.

Her breath caught at the thought. She had been so busy with suspecting Marcy and then Tyler that she had missed perhaps the most obvious suspect of all. While she was off looking for some grand plot or mystery, maybe the answer was really as simple as an angry man who let himself get pushed too far.

"Marcy, can I ask you about Robert? The man who was murdered in the motel room two doors down from yours?"

"Oh, yes, it was horrible," Marcy said. "I didn't know about it until the police showed up at your restaurant. I have no idea what happened or why that other woman thought I did it."

"You didn't hear anything, did you? No arguing or anything like that?"

"No, but I only stopped in my room briefly before leaving again to go to your restaurant. When your employee told me you wouldn't be in for another hour, I spent that time driving around town." She hesitated. "I told this to the police, but not to anyone else. When I checked into the motel, the owner gave me the wrong room number. I let myself in Room 2 and heard the shower running. I was so embarrassed. I called out an apology and hurried back to the office to let him know the room was already occupied. Ever since I learned he was dead, I've been wondering if I could have done something, or if it was my fault somehow. Did I leave the door open? Did I give the killer a way to get to him?"

Lydia supposed that answered her unasked question about the pictures on Nellie's phone. She might not have believed Marcy's explanation if it hadn't been for Jacob's utter lack of care about the motel. He didn't seem like he would care in the slightest if he double booked a room.

"It wasn't your fault," she said. "The only person at fault is whoever killed him—and maybe Jacob, since security at the motel is his responsibility."

If he wasn't personally responsible for the murder, that was.

They kept chatting as Lydia drove, until she finally reached the turn-in for the motel. She hit her blinker and turned into the lot. The vehicle behind her did the same, which was a relief. Hopefully, Jacob would be less likely to do something with another guest there.

The lights were on in the office at the far end of the building, and she felt the hairs on the back of her neck prickle. Had Robert's killer been hiding in plain sight all along? Maybe Robert had complained about the state of his room, or even threatened legal action. She couldn't imagine any of the rooms were in good condition. The police would have questioned Jacob, since he owned the motel, but Nellie's insistence that Marcy was the killer might have thrown them off track.

Now wasn't the time to put things together, though. Right now, she needed to get herself and Marcy as far away from here as possible.

She pulled into the spot next to Marcy's van, ignoring the other vehicle as it pulled in a few spots away and the driver shut the headlights off.

"All right, I parked," Lydia said, picking her phone up and rerouting the call to go through the earpiece instead of her SUV's bluetooth.

"I'm going to undo the chain and the deadbolt," Marcy said as Lydia got out of her vehicle.

"We can lock up again as soon as—"

A bag made of white plastic came down over her head from behind, smothering her when she tried to inhale for a scream and knocking the phone out of her hands. She felt the bag tighten around her neck as the person behind her pulled back on it.

Someone was suffocating her. Dismissing the car that had followed her here might have cost her her life.

THIRTEEN

Time seemed to slow down as Lydia tried to fight off the person who was trying to kill her. She reached behind her, hoping to scratch the person's face, and instead got a handful of long hair. A woman was attacking her. Had Marcy lured her here to kill her?

No. Marcy had been talking on the phone when Lydia got out of the car. She would have heard her if she was in the parking lot, lurking behind Lydia's SUV. And why would Marcy go through all of this effort to lure her back to the motel when they were already planning on meeting tomorrow?

No, the woman had to be Nellie. Nellie had insisted on meeting Lydia instead of talking on the phone and had tried to push the meeting late enough that the restaurant would be empty except for the two of them. She must have been waiting in the parking lot, and followed her here from the restaurant.

But why? Lydia's text telling Nellie she thought she had another suspect for Robert's murder must have been what set her off. Had Nellie killed her own fiancé?

Did she think Lydia had been hinting that she knew the truth?

None of it mattered, because Lydia couldn't breathe, and Nellie had already killed at least one other person, someone who was bigger and stronger than she was. She was going to die in this overgrown parking lot in front of a run-down motel.

Still, Lydia tried to fight the woman off. Nellie wasn't significantly stronger than her, but she had the advantage of not currently being suffocated by a plastic bag, and she managed to dodge or deflect each of Lydia's attempts to free herself.

Then she heard a wordless shout and felt a sharp jerk against her neck—but then the pressure released, and she could yank the plastic garbage bag off her head and breathe again. She gasped in great lungfuls of air and turned around to see Marcy standing between her and Nellie, holding an unplugged table lamp like a club.

"You almost killed her!" Marcy shouted, her voice high-pitched with panic. "Wait, you're that crazy woman from the restaurant. First you accuse me of murder, then you try to kill my sister? What's going on?"

"It's not about you," Lydia said, coughing. "She... I think she's the one who killed Robert. She murdered her own fiancé."

"But ... why try to pin it on me? I didn't have anything to do with it."

"He was cheating on me with you!" Nellie said. She looked like she wanted to get her hands around Marcy's throat this time but was too wary of the lamp Marcy was holding to come closer. "Don't try to deny it. I saw you go into his room."

"Then you would've seen me go right back out. I was given the wrong room number when I checked in."

Nellie faltered. "I ... I didn't want to watch. As soon as I had the pictures, I drove away. You're ... you're lying." She sounded uncertain now, almost afraid.

"I have no idea what your fiancé was doing here, but whatever it was, it wasn't with me," Marcy said. "Lydia, we should call the police. My phone is still in my room. Maybe an ambulance, too. Is your throat all right?"

Nodding, though she was still massaging her throat and enjoying the simple sensation of breathing, Lydia stooped to grab her phone off the ground and handed it to Marcy. She wasn't sure she would be able to get all of the information out without coughing. Marcy pulled up the dial pad and typed in the number, the lamp tucked under her elbow.

"Wait," Nellie said, her voice breaking. "He really wasn't here to meet you?"

"He wasn't cheating on you," Lydia managed to get out. Her voice was a little hoarse, but she was feeling better by the moment. "He was here to collect a debt. He lent money to someone who was having a hard time paying it back. I think he was involved in online gambling, and he was trying to hide it from you. That's why he was being so secretive."

Nellie, who had looked murderous a moment before, looked like her entire world had shattered.

She took a step back, as if she could run away from the truth.

"No, you're lying. That isn't … he would have told me…"

"You thought he was having an affair," Lydia said. "And you killed him for it. Then you tried to pin it on Marcy … and you stuck around to make sure the accusation would stick."

"I thought it would be fitting," Nellie whispered. "I wanted her to suffer for what she did too. When I confronted him, he was so offended that I followed him here. He was mad that I thought he was the sort of person who would have an affair in a seedy motel. I thought he was just being defensive, but he … he was telling the truth. And I killed him. Oh, my goodness. What did I do? He must have been so confused, so scared…"

Nellie started to cry. The murderous woman was gone, replaced by someone who looked utterly broken. Marcy gave Lydia a wide-eyed look, though most of her focus was on the phone call. She was repeating their address to the dispatcher.

The door to the motel's office opened, and Jacob shouted, "What's going on out there? Keep it down!" before slamming the door shut again.

She really hoped this place got closed down for good.

EPILOGUE

"This is it."

"Are you sure you don't want to wait to open it with Lillian?" Jude asked.

They were seated on her couch, Saffron sprawled out on her dog bed in the corner. Lydia had bought it for her weeks ago, and the dog loved it. They had just gone on one of their long hikes, and the first thing Lydia had done was the same thing she had been doing all week—she checked the mail. Finally, the DNA results were here.

She shook her head. "Honestly, we're both convinced by this point. This is just a formality. Even if we're mistaken, we're still going to keep in contact with her. She saved my life, and it was hard for Lillian to believe she was still after my money or my business or my kidney after that."

"But you still want to be sure," he said, understanding.

She took a deep breath. "Yeah. I still want to be sure."

Carefully, she opened the letter and took out the folded paper inside. She unfolded it, looking at an unfamiliar graph of dots and bars, two colors overlaid with each other. She had no idea what it meant, but the text beneath the graph explained it.

Marcy was her half-sister. Their genes didn't lie.

She breathed out, feeling relief she hadn't expected. In the weeks since the incident at the motel, she had gotten to know Marcy quite well. They spoke on the phone almost every day, and they had taken to sharing recipes back and forth. Not ones from the restaurant, but family recipes. It turned out Marcy liked cooking too, though it was a hobby for her and not a career.

"Wow," she breathed. "It's real. I have another sister. Well, half-sister, but as far as I'm concerned, it's the same thing."

"Congratulations," Jude said. He slipped an arm around her shoulders and squeezed, giving her half a hug.

She leaned into him, smiling. "This is so exciting, Jude. I mean, my parents are going to be shocked. Lillian and I will have to talk about how to tell them, but I think they'll both come around. You haven't met them, but they're very easy going. I know my mom had some crazy college adventures too, so she can't blame my dad for this. It's not his fault Marcy's mother never told him."

"I'm happy for you," he said. "I know this has been weighing on you for the last few weeks."

"It had. I feel like things can finally start getting back to normal now."

"Well in that case…"

He took his arm from around her shoulders and sat up straighter, suddenly nervous. "I've been wanting to ask you for a while, but the time never seemed right. We've had a crazy few months. But with things a little calmer now… I'd like to take you on a date. My treat, I'll take you anywhere you want. If you say no, I'll never bring it up again. I don't want this to derail our friendship."

Her stomach fluttered. "I've been trying to find the perfect time to ask *you* on a date," she said. "It's a definite yes. I'm happy to go anywhere other than Iron and Flame. This is the first real date I've gone on in years, and I do not need my ex-husband making us dinner during it."

He laughed, draping his arm across her shoulders again. "That sounds reasonable to me. I'll do some research and see if I can find a good restaurant that's new to us both."

She had a date to look forward to, and not one but *two* sisters to call and share the news with. It was hard to believe that just under a year ago, her life had consisted of nothing more than days spent at the restaurant and nights spent alone in her bland little rented house. Right now, her world seemed so full it could burst.

Printed in Great Britain
by Amazon